The Horse, the Stars, and the Road

Lucy Kelly-Desmond

THE HORSE, THE STARS AND THE ROAD
First published in 2022 by
Little Island Books
7 Kenilworth Park
Dublin 6w
Ireland

First published in the USA by Little Island Books in 2023

Art direction by Claire Brankin
Design and typesetting by Fintan Wall
Printed in the UK by CPI

Print ISBN: 9781912417896
Little Island has received funding to support this book from the Arts Council of Ireland

10 9 8 7 6 5 4 3 2 1

For my parents
and dedicated to the memory of
Thomas O'Reilly,
a guiding star in the night sky

On the way home from school,
the children are planning their projects.

Everyone has to bring something in from home
after the break.

Aleksander can't wait to teach everyone
some Polish words.
Gracie is going to wear her Nigerian dress.

I suppose I could bring in a horseshoe,
Sonny thinks.
But maybe people would think that was boring.

At home, Sonny tells Dad about the project.
'Simon's cousin found a Bronze-Age axe-head on
their farm. Simon is going to bring in a photo of it.'

'We'll think of something, Sonny,' Dad says,
'when you get back from your trip.'

Sonny watches out of the window
until Uncle Jim arrives.

'Are you ready for the road?' Jim asks.

Kathleen is coming too, and Puddles the
dog. But Dad is staying at home.

Sonny and Puddles sit inside the wagon
while they travel through the streets.

They leave the city far behind.

There are no shops now, and no street lights.

There aren't even any electricity poles.

When it gets dark, the stars come out.

Jim tells Sonny that people who know the stars can find their way in the dark.

'People have been doing that for thousands of years,' he says.

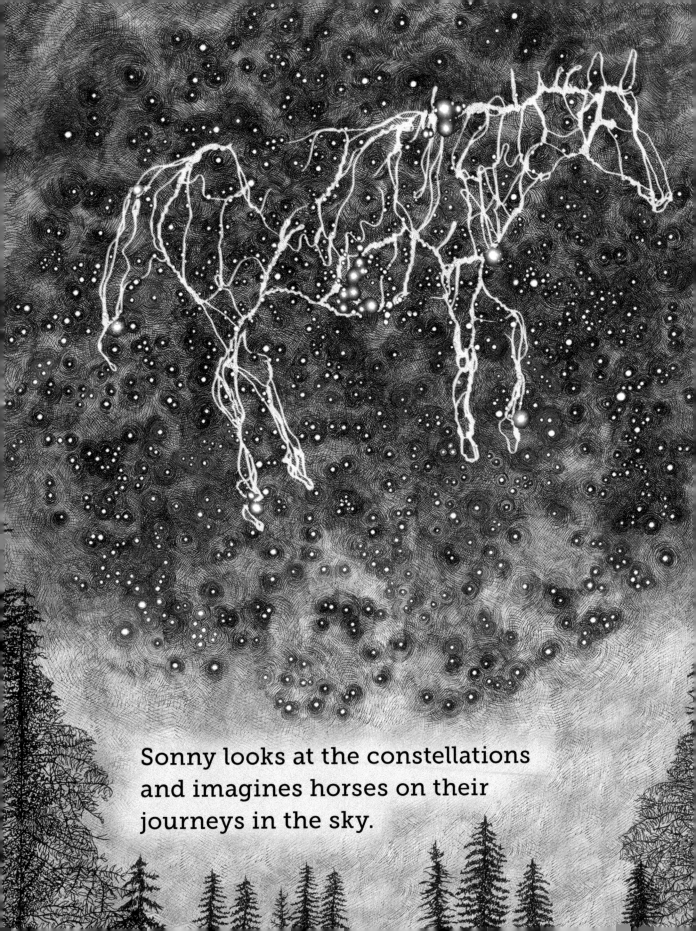

Sonny looks at the constellations and imagines horses on their journeys in the sky.

At the campsite, Jim tells Sonny,
Kathleen, and Puddles stories
about his childhood.
Sonny loves that.

Jim knows how to do
all kinds of things.

His father taught him...

and his father
taught him...

... and so on back
for generations.

Jim takes them to a horse fair.

Sonny has never felt so proud
to be a Traveller.

Back at the camp, Sonny helps Jim with the horses and donkeys.

The horse who pulls their wagon is called Peggy.

They are going home tomorrow.

Sonny feels very lonely as they make their way back to the city.

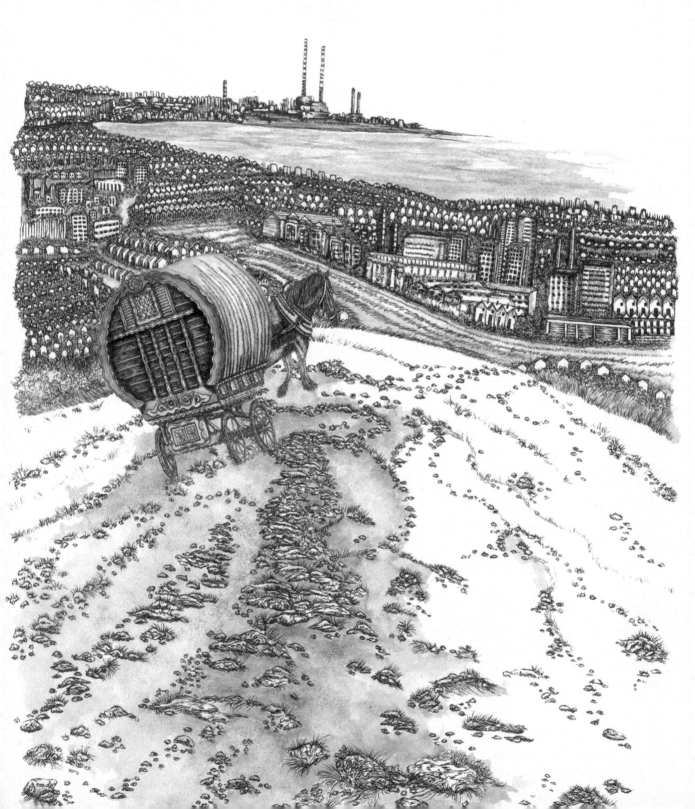

As Sonny strokes Peggy one last
time, he feels like crying.

He runs into the house
without looking back.

Later on, Kathleen comes into
Sonny's room with a present for him –
something shimmering, the colour
of fire.

'Uncle Jim made a special kind of
lantern just for you, Sonny,' she says.

Until you join me on
the road again;
sleep soundly
under the stars

Slowly, the carousel begins to spin.
The light inside it flickers like the campfire.

Stars twinkle on the ceiling and horses go trotting across the walls of Sonny's room.

Sonny can't wait to show his classmates
the wonderful thing his uncle,
the tinsmith, has made.

He even feels a bit sorry for Simon
with his picture of an axe-head.

Acknowledgements

I want to thank the following people for their support and encouragement: The publishing team at Little Island Books—especially Claire Brankin, Elizabeth Goldrick and Siobhán Parkinson.

Special thanks to Leanne McDonagh, Sarah Webb, Christyan Fox, Margrete Lamond and my friend Sue Basler.

About the Artist

Lucy Kelly-Desmond studied textile design and later took a course in children's book illustration. This is her first book.

Although she spent her early years in London, Lucy always thought she was Irish. But when her family moved back to Ireland and she started school at age four, her classmates did not always accept her as Irish. When she was eight, twin sisters, who were Travellers, joined her class. They were used to defending people who didn't quite fit in, and they soon became her friends. They, and their siblings and cousins from other classes, used to tell her about their traditions, and Lucy came to love Traveller culture.

The girls' dad would collect them from school on his horse-drawn cart, which could be heard coming down the street. Lucy remembers a school project where everyone had to draw their home and family. The teacher told the twins to include their horse and cart in the drawings. Lucy longed to be able to draw something as wonderful for her project.

Lucy's family later moved to Ballinasloe, in the west of Ireland, where Europe's oldest horse fair takes place every October. As an art student, Lucy was invited to take photographs and do drawings of the O'Reilly family's barrel top wagon – the last wagon to set up camp on Fair Hill. This rekindled her love of Traveller culture, and after watching one of the last tinsmiths working at the fair, she made a copper lantern carousel and an idea for this story was formed.

About Little Island

Little Island is an independent Irish publisher that looks for the best writing for young readers, in Ireland and internationally. Founded in 2010 by Ireland's inaugural Laureate na nÓg (Children's Laureate), Little Island has published over 100 books, many of which have won awards and been published in translation around the world.